MARGARET GREAVES

JUNIPER'S JOURNEY

Illustrated by Joanna Carey

Methuen Children's Books

*For Gill and
another Juniper*

First published in Great Britain 1990
by Methuen Children's Books
Michelin House, 81 Fulham Road, London SW3 6RB
Text copyright © 1990 Margaret Greaves
Illustrations copyright © 1990 Joanna Carey
Printed in Great Britain by St Edmundsbury Press,
Bury St Edmunds, Suffolk

British Library Cataloguing in Publication Data

Greaves, Margaret .
Juniper's Journey.
I. Title   II. Carey, Joanna
823.914

ISBN 0–416–15572–3

Contents

For Gill,

With love and all good wishes,

Margaret.

April 1990

JUNIPER'S JOURNEY

CHAPTER ONE

Alone

She had no name. No one had cared enough to give her one. Without a name it's very hard to feel that you are a real person.

'Never expect anything from people,' her mother told her. 'Then you won't be disappointed.'

There was a deep sadness inside her mother. It was not a sadness about anything in particular. It was just that the injustice of the world against donkeys had sunk deep into her soul and showed in her eyes.

But the little she-foal found it hard to believe her. She knew already about blows and hunger. But when she grazed beside her mother, when the sun shone and the young grass shivered in the wind, she was almost sure that there must be something else as well, something better. She didn't know what or where it was, but some day she would find it.

Two or three times a week Fred Staple would harness the foal's mother to a cart filled with vegetables to sell in the nearby town. Helped by his son, Eric, he made a poor sort of living from his market garden. He was a rough, bitter-tempered man, with little sympathy for anyone. The foal galloped away whenever he fetched her mother from the field. She could see her soon afterwards struggling against the weight of the heavy cart on the steep lane that led down to the road. Hours later she would come back utterly weary, urged up the hill by the thwack of a heavy stick.

The little foal dreaded days like this, and was lonely when her mother was gone. Fred's wife, thin and work-worn, had no time to spare for animals. But sometimes Dawn, who was still at school, would bring a windfall apple or a broken carrot, offered with a pat and a word of casual kindness. But in that first spring, on the few days when her mother stayed in the field, the foal was sometimes quite happy.

The late summer was unusually hot. The grass burned yellow, and grazing was thin and poor. The mother donkey's milk dried up, and she and her foal were often hungry. The vegetable harvest suffered, and Fred Staple said that he couldn't afford to buy extra food for animals.

'Will it always be like this?' asked the little foal.

'No,' said her mother. 'There is still the winter to come.'

'What is winter?'

The old donkey's hide twitched and shivered in spite of the heat.

'It is dreadful,' she said. 'Rain and wind, or bitter cold. And the grass sometimes hidden by snow or iron-hard with frost. My little one, I wish you need never know what winter is.'

But her wish was not granted. The little foal grew bigger and stronger although she was so often hungry. The September mists came and went, and October set in with heavy rain. Late in November the frosts began to bite. Soon the ground was so hard that to trot over it was like trotting on the stony lane outside.

Fred's temper grew worse. One January morning he loaded the cart and harnessed the donkey to it. She threw her weight against the collar, braced all her muscles, and pulled. Nothing moved. The wheels were stuck fast in a deep layer of half-frozen mud and slush. Fred's stick thudded across her back.

'Git on wi' it! Git!'

The donkey heaved again, desperately. The cart shifted very slightly, then stuck. Once again the heavy stick fell, and sweat made a dark stain on her flanks.

'The old moke can't 'elp it,' protested Eric. 'Wheels are stuck against summat. 'Dawn! Dawn!' he shouted towards the house. 'Come on out. You're wanted.'

With the three of them pushing behind, the cart at last lurched forward. The donkey, urged again by the stick, broke into a trot. She was going too fast as she swung into the lane. A few yards down the slush had melted and then frozen overnight into a smooth grey patch. The donkey braced her forefeet, but the weight of the heavy cart pushed her forward. She tried to throw herself back on her haunches, but the load was too much for her to hold. Her knees gave way and she came down in a tangle of harness. Boxes of vegetables spilled out into the lane.

Fred's sullen temper broke out into a blaze. He had given the donkey two or three cruel blows before Eric ran after him and caught his arm.

"Er can't get up till you've loosed 'er,' he said. 'We'll 'ave to unbuckle 'er first.'

The donkey lay a long time on the freezing ground before the harness was disentangled, the vegetables picked up, and the two men hauled her to her feet. From the field the foal watched with frightened eyes.

The cart returned later than usual. It had been a bad day. Only half the load had been sold, and the donkey could hardly manage the final drag up the hill.

The night was the coldest of the winter. The foal huddled close against her mother for warmth. Grudgingly Fred had given them a small feed of hay. It was sour and smelled of damp, but the foal ate her share hungrily. Her mother would not touch it. Every now and then she broke into violent shivering. Her nose was hot and her breathing heavy and laboured. When the tired foal lay down, her mother stayed on her feet. She too was very tired, but any pressure against her side would increase the pain in it.

When Eric came to harness her next morning, he found her with neck outstretched to ease her breathing. There were damp staring patches on her ragged coat.

'The moke's sick,' he told his father anxiously. 'We'll 'ave to rest 'er today.'

'Sick?' growled Fred. 'Bone lazy, more like. We can't afford a beast that won't work.'

But he noticed the heave of the donkey's flanks and gave her a lighter load than usual. All the same it took every ounce of her strength to draw it. Every now and then she gave a hoarse painful cough.

The foal heard the stumbling sound of her feet as she came back later in the day. She ran to the hedge to look for her. Her mother was coming up the lane very slowly.

'Git on! Git on!' shouted Fred impatiently, striking her almost by habit.

The donkey made a desperate plunge. But the cough took her again. She staggered, her knees giving way beneath her, and fell with out-stretched neck and sprawling legs. Once again the stick fell, but this time she seemed not to feel it.

She lay quite still.

Somehow the foal knew she would never get up again. And after a while she opened her mouth in a shrill protesting bray and galloped away over the empty field.

CHAPTER TWO

Tinker

Now the foal was utterly alone. No one came near her. She was too young to work yet. The men seemed to forget her, and even Dawn hardly ever came. She thought of the donkey only when it suited her.

The foal roamed the poor pasture, browsing for what she could find. Sometimes, when she remembered her mother or when the wind raked coldly against her ribs, she would lift her head and bray her sorrows aloud. But still she dreamed that there must be something else beyond the loneliness and that one day she would find it.

Fred and his son now humped their vegetables to the bottom of the lane. There they were picked up by a good-natured neighbour who was ready to help out for a bit. The weather had changed and the frost given way at last.

One evening, just before dusk, the foal heard the clip-clop of shod hooves in the lane. She pricked up her big soft ears and trotted over to investigate. The gate from the yard swung open to let in a small bay pony. Eric slipped off its headstall and shut the gate behind it.

Interested and hopeful, the foal trotted towards the newcomer. Then she hesitated, shy and uncertain since he took no notice of her. He just stood for a moment with drooping head and then began to graze. The foal remembered how

her mother had sometimes come back too tired even to greet her. So she stood where she was and watched until the field faded into darkness.

She was woken from sleep next morning by the sound of munching. The bay pony was quite close. In the sharp early daylight she could see the deep hollows above his eyes and the roughness of his coat. He lifted his head to stare at her, then pricked his ears. Encouraged, the foal took a step or two nearer, stretching out her neck. The two soft muzzles met. It was a tentative and cautious greeting, but not unfriendly.

'You're young to be on your own,' said the newcomer. 'Where's your mother?'

The foal twitched uneasily.

'She fell. They took her away. She didn't come back.'

'That's bad.' The pony blew softly through his nose. 'Why did she fall?'

'The road was icy. And the cart was so heavy.'

'Hmmm,' snorted the pony. 'That's why they bought me then. To do her work.'

The foal was sorry. She liked her new companion and she could see that he was old. She didn't want him to be treated as her mother had been.

'I'm called Tinker. What's your name?' asked the pony after a long silence.

'I haven't got a name,' said the foal forlornly.
'Not even a name! That's bad too.'

The pony moved nearer and arched his neck
above hers. She felt comforted for the first time
since she was left alone. They stood in silence
for a long while.

Then the field gate clashed, and the foal
wheeled and galloped away as Fred came near.
But Tinker allowed himself to be caught quite

easily and submitted quietly to being harnessed. He was still sturdy and the loaded cart was not too much for him, even though Fred now sat in it to drive. The foal was relieved to see him making a steady pace down the lane without any touch of the whip.

She and Tinker were soon close friends. However tired he was when he came home he was always pleased to see her again. Sometimes he would tell her stories of his past life. Some of the memories were happy, but not all. The foal shivered.

'I don't think I want to grow up,' she said in a very small voice.

'Cheer up, Big Ears,' said Tinker. 'It isn't always bad.'

The foal was pleased whenever he called her Big Ears. It was the nearest thing to a name she'd ever had.

'There's decent owners as well as bad ones,' went on Tinker. 'And the better you work the less likely you are to have trouble.'

The foal sighed. It didn't seem a very cheerful prospect.

'Don't you think,' she asked timidly, 'that perhaps somewhere there is Something Else?'

The pony's wise old eyes were puzzled.

'What sort of something else?'

But the foal hardly knew herself what she

meant, so she didn't answer. She never asked about the Something Else again, but she never forgot it.

As the summer wore on she was contented enough. But soon it was autumn. The grass stopped growing and the grazing was poor. By November the pony was sometimes taken into the shed in the yard and given some hay. But there was none for the little donkey left in the field.

'I can't afford feed for a useless animal,' grumbled Fred Staple. "Er'll 'ave to go. We can sell 'er at the next Lydd Fair.'

'Oh no, Dad!' Dawn was quite upset. She liked the young donkey well enough in weather when it was nice to wander in the fields. 'She don't eat much. And she's company for Tinker.'

A thoughtful greedy look spread over Fred's face.

'If you want 'er so much, my girl, you can 'elp 'er earn 'er keep. I've an idea.'

In the next two or three weeks there was a lot of hammering heard from the shed in the yard.

Then one morning Eric came into the field with a halter in his hand. He ignored Tinker and, to the donkey's great surprise, came over to her instead. She flung up her head, watchful and nervous. He could almost touch her when she wheeled in fright and galloped away down the

18

field. Fred swore and chased her, while she dodged and circled. But he was more experienced than she was, and he was driving her nearer and nearer to a corner of the field. He was growing angry, too, and at last he picked up a stone and threw it. It struck her painfully on the ribs so that she gasped and checked, and next moment the halter was round her neck. She fought uselessly to resist as she was dragged into the yard.

A cart was waiting there, much smaller than the one that Tinker drew. It was empty and not very heavy. Fred forced her back roughly between the shafts while Eric fastened the unfamiliar harness.

At first, terrified and not understanding, her left side still aching from the stone, she refused to move. But Fred's heavy stick came down hard across her rump until little by little she gave way. She was scared by the unfamiliar thing bumping behind her, but she drew it round and round the yard until she got used to it.

When she got back to the field Eric tethered her by a long rope attached to a heavy peg in the ground. He wasn't going to have trouble in catching her again next morning. Tinker tried to comfort her.

'It was sure to happen at last,' he told her. 'It's what we're born to – though you're too young yet for real work. A lot they care about that! But do as they want. Then you won't get hurt so much.'

In a day or two she was used to the noise and movement of the cart behind her. Then one morning she found that Dawn was standing beside it, looking very sulky. She was more shabbily dressed than usual, in grubby jeans and a thin jacket. She looked peaked and cold. Her hair was scraped back and tied into a pony-tail, making her look younger than she was. The cart was filled with boxes of vegetables. Fred came out to them, grinning.

'No need to scowl like that, my girl. Plenty of kids 'ave 'oliday jobs. It's time you both did a bit o' work to pay for your keep. Good thing you're so small and skinny! You'd easily pass for ten. The poor little girl and 'er poor little donkey! Wring their 'earts, you will. I reckon you'll get plenty of Christmas boxes.'

Now, for the first time, the little donkey felt the full weight of the loaded cart. It was far less than that of the big one to which Tinker was already harnessed. But she was barely half-grown yet and it took all her strength to get it moving. The pony whinnied encouragement as he went ahead of her, and she tried to remember his advice.

Her legs already ached when they reached the town and she learned what her work was to be.

While Fred Staple drove to the local shops and other regular customers, Dawn led her cart round the small back streets. Her father was right. Many housewives were indeed sorry for the poor little girl and her poor little donkey. They sometimes bought vegetables just to show their sympathy, and often gave Dawn a bit more than she asked for them. Some of them saved apples or carrots or lumps of sugar for the donkey. Hungry as she was, she took them very gently, and felt better when kind hands sometimes caressed her.

But the daily load was still too heavy for young bones and muscles. Her hooves, never yet trimmed, were uncomfortable too. And, however much she rolled when she came home, she could never get rid of the misery and irritation of the lice in her tangled fur.

Sometimes she still thought that there must be something else, but it seemed to be further and further away.

CHAPTER THREE

Christmas Eve

Soon the streets of the little town began to look very cheerful. Small green trees, covered with tiny lights, appeared in the windows of houses. There were big ones above some of the shops and a huge one in the Square. Strings of lights hung above the main road as well. Everyone seemed in good humour. The little donkey received more apples and sugar than usual. People wished each other a happy Christmas. The donkey didn't know what Christmas was, but she hoped it would go on for a long time.

Not that her own life was any better. Her back ached always now, as well as her legs. There was a raw place where the harness had rubbed but no one had noticed. The journey to the town seemed longer every day.

'Christmas Eve,' Fred said to his daughter. 'We'll finish early today. My last call is at Jenkins' in East Street. I've promised 'im another

bag of sprouts. Meet me there and I'll buy you some sweets from the shop next door. After all, it's Christmas.'

The little donkey had never seen him so nearly amiable.

It was half-past two when Dawn led her into East Street and they stopped outside Mr Jenkins' shop. The sign over the door – FAMILY GROCER: FRUIT AND VEGETABLES – was garlanded with holly and the shop looked bright and inviting. Fred's cart was already there and Mr Jenkins was paying for his sprouts. Fred looked round.

"Ere she is,' he said. 'That's my kid, that is.'

Mr Jenkins looked hard at Dawn as he greeted her, and hard at the donkey as well.

'That donkey's young to be working,' he said.

'She's all right,' said Fred defensively. 'She may be little, but she's strong.'

Mr Jenkins said nothing to this, but told them

to wait while he got something for the little girl. In a minute he came out again with a bag of nuts and a packet of chocolate for Dawn. He had a carrot for the donkey, too. And while she munched it he ran his hands gently over her and down her legs, making soft friendly sounds.

'She's a nice little beast,' he said. 'You won't be able to work her, will you, when the child's at school again?'

A cunning look came into Fred's eyes.

'Right enough. But the girl's that fond of 'er, I 'as to keep 'er, see. Though it's not easy on what I earn. You love 'er, don't you, Dawn?'

'Yes, Dad,' said Dawn, catching his sideways look at her.

She put an arm round the donkey's neck and made a great show of rubbing and kissing her nose. The donkey's ears flickered as Dawn's hair tickled her nostrils, and she shifted her feet uneasily. She was unused to this kind of attention.

'If you're fond of her, you'd like her to have a good home, wouldn't you?' asked the grocer. 'Where she wouldn't have to work so hard. She'd do splendidly for my little chap. He needs a pet to look after. I'll give you a fair price for her.'

'Well, I'm sure I don't know.' Fred brought a whine into his voice. 'It's an 'ard choice for a poor man to make. What d'you think, Dawn?'

Dawn had her father's sense of a bargain. She hid her face against the grey furry neck and muttered. 'I don't want her to go.'

'I tell you what,' said Mr Jenkins. 'There's a good second-hand bike at the back of the shop. Your daughter can have it for Christmas – on top of the price for the donkey.'

Dawn dropped her hands quickly and looked up, hopeful and greedy. A donkey was nothing compared with a bike of her own.

'A bike?'

'It's yours if your father'll sell the donkey.'

'Dad?'

Fred looked thoughtful and pretended to hesitate. But he knew the price offered was a good one. And when the school holiday was over the bike would certainly be more use than the donkey.

'Well,' he said with pretended reluctance, 'seeing it's you, Mr Jenkins – and for a little kiddie –'

So in a few minutes it was settled. The grocer handed over some money, then fetched the bike. They unharnessed the donkey, loaded the small cart into the big one that was now empty, and put the bike on top of it. Dawn climbed up without a glance at her recent 'friend'. Before the donkey understood what had happened, she saw Tinker clattering off down the street with his two passengers seated behind him.

She stretched out her neck in a long loud desolate bray. She had been left in a strange place with a stranger, while her only real friend in the world trotted away out of her life.

'There now, there's no need for that,' said Mr Jenkins comfortingly. 'I'd say you're well rid of that precious pair. You'd better wait round the back till I've finished. It's quieter there.'

He led her down a passage at the side of the shop, into a small yard behind it. It was cluttered with boxes, broken crates and sacks of rubbish. But a narrow roof ran along one side, and beneath it the donkey was protected from the wind.

It seemed to her a long time that she waited there alone. Her stomach ached with hunger. Tit-bits didn't make a meal. She was puzzled, nervous, and had never wanted Tinker's company so much. But at last there were footsteps in the passage, and a friendly hand on her neck as Mr Jenkins untied her.

'Home now,' he said, talking simply to soothe her by the sound of his voice. 'It's all fixed up for you. Bert Pratt says you're welcome to stay in his field, and he'll let us have some feed as well until we can get some in.'

Still scared by the unknown, the donkey

braced herself stubbornly against him. But instead of the expected blow she felt only a friendly clap on the neck.

'Come on now, little 'un. Nothing's going to hurt you. You've had a bad time, I can see, but things'll be better now.'

Encouraged by his tone she let herself be led along the passage, past the front of the shop, down a side lane, until they came to the gate of a field. Mr Jenkins led her through it and down to the nearest corner where there was a small open shed.

'Bert's a good chap. He's left you some grub already, I see. Be easy now. I'll see you tomorrow.'

He slipped the rope from her neck, gave her a friendly rub down her nose, and left her.

The donkey hesitated, afraid of the unknown. But a warm enticing smell floated towards her from the shed. Very cautiously she walked towards it. Her hooves sank into fresh straw. And there in the corner, tickling her nostrils with its promise, was a heap of clean dry hay.

Hours later the little donkey woke to the clear starry darkness of a winter morning. The air shook with the sound of bells. She had heard them only faintly before, drifting in snatches on the wind up to the high hill field where she had been born. But here the noise was all around her, rollicking cascades of it that touched her with a little shiver of excitement. She threw up her head and brayed back at the bells, then flung into a gallop all round the field.

As the darkness thinned into daylight she began to wonder what would happen next. She went back into the shed and munched some of the hay that was left.

At last the gate creaked and footsteps crunched over the crisp grass. She took a pace or two forward to look, then waited anxiously. She recognised Mr Jenkins. Beside him, clutching his hand, trotted a small boy.

'I've got something to show you,' Mr Jenkins was saying. 'Look! Just inside the shed.'

The boy ran forward, then stopped, staring at her.

'It's a donkey! A donkey! Where's it come from?'

'She's *your* donkey,' said his father. 'Happy Christmas, Colin! She's your Christmas present.'

'*Mine?*' The boy stared at him, breathless, hardly daring to believe. 'Mine?'

Mr Jenkins laughed. 'Certainly yours. But she's been badly treated. You'll have to be careful with her.'

The boy ran forward, glowing with excitement. Startled, remembering how Eric

had chased her, she flinched and swerved aside.
At once he stood still, dropping his hands to his
sides.

'It's all right. It's all right. There's nothing to
be scared of.'

The voice was gentle, coaxing, unlike those
she usually heard. The habit of fear inside her
gave way a little. She cocked her ears to listen,
then made a cautious step towards him. The boy
waited patiently, still without moving. Another
step. Another. And then she was close enough
for him to reach out a quiet hand to stroke her
neck and muzzle. Next moment his arm was

round her neck and his cheek against it. Dawn's careless touch had never been like this.

'Oh Dad, *look!*' Colin still spoke softly for fear of scaring her again. 'She's lovely. Lovely.'

'She'll look much better when the vet's had a look at her and you've given her a bit of care.'

'Can I ride her today, Dad?'

'Sorry, son, but not yet. Not for a long time. Donkeys shouldn't be worked at her age. Her bones and muscles still have to get strong. But you can look after her and train her until she's ready.'

Colin's face fell for a moment. He had pictured himself as riding that very day. Then he looked at his new friend's tangled coat, the rubbed sore patches on her thin ribs, and stifled his disappointment.

'It doesn't matter,' he said. 'I'll ride her when she's bigger. Oh Dad, she's the gorgeousest Christmas present I've ever had. I bet no one else has had a donkey for Christmas!'

'I'm glad you're pleased,' smiled his father. 'What will you call her?'

Colin stood back and studied her.

'You could call her Eeyore,' suggested Mr Jenkins.

'Eeyore was a he,' said Colin rather crushingly. He thought for a minute. 'Perhaps – perhaps – Noel. Because she's a Christmas donkey.' He tried it out. 'Noel. Noel. No, that's not right . . .'

Suddenly his face cleared.

'Juniper,' he said. 'That's what she is. Juniper. Look, she likes it.'

The little donkey's ears had flicked forward and she was pressing her soft nose into his chest. She was trembling with joy. At last she had a name. A real name all to herself. She was Juniper.

All at once she knew what had happened. There *was* something else. And she had found it.

CHAPTER FOUR

Something Else

That first day in her new home was the most wonderful that Juniper had ever known. Colin brought her carrots and apples as a Christmas present, his eyes shining with love and delight. His hands and voice gentled her. He squatted comfortably beside her in the dry straw and talked.

'You're a special donkey,' he told her. 'A Christmas donkey. All donkeys are a bit special because the ox and ass kept the baby warm in the stable at Bethlehem. But you are *extra* special because you're a Christmas present.'

Juniper didn't understand the words, but she understood the tone. And for the first time in her life she felt that she really *was* special. She put her head over Colin's shoulder and kept it there, breathing affection. This, she thought to herself, must be happiness. It was a strange feeling, but good.

A day or two later Mr Jenkins and Colin came into the field with a young woman who carried a black case. Juniper watched her uncertainly. But Colin was talking happily to her – perhaps it was all right. She allowed Mr Jenkins to fasten a headstall and a leading rein, and stood quietly while the strange lady stroked and talked to her.

Firm but kind hands explored the donkey's back and legs, sometimes finding the raw places where she had rubbed her back too hard against a fence to relieve the itching of her skin. Colin watched closely and anxiously. At last the stranger straightened up.

'There's no permanent injury to the back, I think. Nothing that rest won't cure. And those sores will heal when we've got rid of the lice. I'll give you some powder for those. Now, Colin, I need your help. Walk her forward a bit. Slowly.'

Proudly, Colin took the leading rein and patted the donkey's thin neck.

'Come on, Juniper. Let Miss Thorne look at you.'

Trustingly she followed him, forwards and back.

'Now at a trot,' said the vet. 'Good. Not much wrong there. You've rescued her in time. She'll be a fine little beast one day. Good food, shelter and love, that's all she really needs. I'll send the farrier in a day or two to trim those hooves.'

'Will he let me help him?' asked Colin.

'I'm sure he will. You seem to have a way with animals. In any case you can hold her and watch how he does it.'

'Oh good! I want to be a vet one day,' said Colin, 'so I've got to learn all I can.'

'Good luck then,' smiled Miss Thorne. 'If you

still feel the same in a few years' time, let me know. I can sometimes do with an assistant in school holiday time.'

Before he could thank her she moved away, talking to Mr Jenkins, but Colin lingered.

'Oh, Juniper, I do love you! You'll be all right now. No one's going to ill-treat you again. Not ever.'

Juniper believed him. Everything made her feel safe and protected. Every day there was food. Not too much at first, until her half-starved stomach was ready to take it. But before long her sides filled out, her sores healed. Colin groomed her carefully every day, and when the ingrained dirt and tangled hair were at last combed away, the vet was proved right. She was indeed a beautiful donkey. Her hide was silver-grey, with the long thin black cross down her back which is the mark of all her kind. There was elegance in her slender legs and small delicate hooves.

Often Colin would lead her out of the field for a walk along the lanes. People would stop to talk to her and admire her, and she made many friends. She loved these outings which satisfied the one thing that she still lacked. She hardly knew it herself, but she was lonely in the big field when Colin was at school or busy with other things. Sometimes she would stand for a long hour or two by her favourite bit of hedge – a nice thorny bit of hedge with a thistly patch of rough grass beneath it – but forget even to nibble. She would just stand there, not thinking, not dozing, but with a queer vacant feeling inside her.

The spring turned into summer. One evening there was a disturbance in the next field. The distant gate creaked, heavy hooves thudded suddenly over the grass, a shrill neigh startled all the birds in the hedge. Juniper heard Bert Pratt's voice, loud and cheerful.

'There you go, my beauty. No more work for you for a while. You've earned a rest.'

Into Juniper's view galloped an old black shire horse. Despite his age and bulk he pranced like a two-year-old, whickering with joy at his freedom. The sun reflected from the great curve of his haunches, he flung up clods of earth behind him, and tossed his head as proudly as any thoroughbred. Twice he circled his field, then halted quite close to Juniper. His flanks were heaving with so much exercise.

Juniper pushed her big head over a low bit of the hedge. She felt shy and small in front of this enormous stranger, but was so excited that she had to speak.

'Hello,' she said timidly.

The stranger turned his head towards her and

cocked a friendly ear. At first he looked too high, then lowered his gaze.

'Hello. Oh, there you are. Not much of you, is there?'

'I suppose not. I'm only a donkey, you see.' She nibbled at an imaginary itch on her shoulder to hide her embarrassment. Then she remembered that she was special – Colin said so – and that she had a name, a real name of her own.

'My name's Juniper,' she said proudly. 'What's yours?'

'H-h-h-Hector,' breathed the big horse. 'H-h-h-Hector.' He snatched a mouthful or two of grass. 'Hmmm . . . Nice grass round here.'

'Yes,' agreed Juniper happily. 'Good thistles too.'

She began to nibble them. The excitement had made her hungry. They both munched on in friendly silence, each feeling the closeness of the other, until the long summer shadows melted into dusk.

CHAPTER FIVE

Fresh Fields

'Good morning!' said Juniper, pushing her nose over the low bit of hedge.

'Hmmm. Hmmmm. Good morning to you, little 'un,' snorted Hector.

He had been in the next field for a week now. Juniper liked him. He was big and gentle and quiet. She wished they could share the same field. But just now she had something else on her mind.

'There aren't many thistles left in this corner,' she told him regretfully.

'Thistles? Funny taste you've got,' brooded Hector. 'Plenty of good grass on your side, isn't there?'

'Grass is all right,' agreed Juniper. 'But donkeys like thistles best. They're more scrunchy.'

'Hmmm,' breathed the big horse. 'Plenty of those in the ditch this side. Can't say I care for them myself.'

Juniper scraped a restless foot along the patch of dried mud where she was standing. The hedge here was so thin that it had been patched with strands of wire. The mud crumbled and broke under her hoof. She went on pawing at it absently while she thought – sometimes about how nice it was to have Hector as a neighbour, and sometimes about the thistles in his field. A fly worried her and she rubbed herself against the wire to get rid of it. The wire bent as she pressed against it.

It was then that the idea came to her.

She scraped busily at the bare ground until she had made quite a hollow in it. Then she put her head beneath the bottom strand of wire and pushed.

'What are you doing?' asked Hector with interest.

'You'll see,' promised Juniper.

She rolled on her back in the dry hollow, flattening the earth still more. Then she pushed her head under the wire again, braced her strong neck and shoulders, and heaved. The wire lifted. Another roll, another heave, and suddenly she was through. The loosened wire sagged back again behind her.

'*Now* where are those thistles?' she demanded.

They were delicious. Much scrunchier, she

thought, than those in her own field. She had a lovely morning, sometimes munching, sometimes thinking, sometimes just standing nose to nose with Hector, enjoying the drowsy warmth of the sun.

Late in the afternoon she heard Colin calling

her name. He always came to her as soon as he'd finished his tea after school.

'Juniper! Juniper! *Juniper!*'

At last he reached the boundary hedge, looked across, and saw her.

'Juniper! How on *earth* did you get there? You naughty girl!'

The little donkey flicked her ears in greeting, but stayed obstinately where she was.

'I'll have to get Dad,' said Colin, when all his coaxing failed. 'You just wait till he catches you!'

Juniper ignored the threat. She had perfect faith that no one in her new home would ever hurt her. Soon she heard Mr Jenkins' footsteps, with Colin's, coming along the lane and then into the main road for the gate into Hector's field. Suddenly excited, she tossed her head and broke away into a gallop.

'Well, I never! The little wretch!' said Mr Jenkins. 'Here, girl, here! No fooling now!'

Juniper did a little dance, just for the fun of it. But she loved Colin and she hadn't seen him all day. She let herself be caught at last and led back to her own field.

'Beats me how she got there,' said Mr Jenkins. 'There's no open gate-way, and she's far too small to jump that hedge.'

If donkeys could smile, Juniper would have smiled to herself. She rubbed her nose affectionately against Colin's shoulder and said nothing.

Next morning Bert Pratt fetched Hector away to do a day's carting. The old horse was really retired, but he could still do a job now and then and enjoyed working with his master. It was a dull, still sort of day. There was nothing to excite Juniper, and in any case she'd found another patch of thistles that she'd overlooked in her own field. So she stayed peacefully where she was, fully occupied.

But twice more in that week and once in the next she rolled her way into her friend's field for company. Then came a day of heavy showers that softened all the mud. When Mr Jenkins caught her after the fourth escape, her silver hide was brown and plastered with it. And when he examined the boundary hedge again he found her small hoof-prints on either side of the thin patch, and the marks of a slide between them.

'So *that's* how she did it!' he exclaimed. 'Look, there's mud on that bottom wire as well. The clever little monkey! Who'd have thought she could do it!'

'She's the cleverest donkey in the world,' agreed Colin admiringly. 'But I suppose we'll have to mend the fence now, won't we?'

'We certainly shall. I could do with a creature a bit *less* clever,' grumbled Mr Jenkins. 'But if

she's so keen to get into Hector's field I reckon she must be lonely. She wants her pal. I'll have a word with Bert Pratt about it.

So it was that Juniper found herself sharing the next-door field with Hector, to the great satisfaction of them both. She and Colin continued to grow up together. At nearly four years old she was a beautiful creature, with a friendly trusting nature. Colin was very proud of her.

'She'd compare well now with any donkey in the county,' declared Mr Jenkins. 'And it's about time to train her for some light work. You can begin to ride her, Colin. I'll see about a saddle for her next week. You might even show her next year.'

Juniper was puzzled and suspicious of the saddle at first, and was startled when she first felt Colin's light weight on her back. But as he never hurried her schooling and was always gentle, she soon enjoyed their lessons as much as he did. They were each as proud as the other when, for the first time, they left the field and went out for a ride on their own.

CHAPTER SIX

Routing the Enemy

Now that he could ride her, Colin often took Juniper with him when he was exploring the nearby fields and woods. He was passionately interested in wild creatures of every kind. His mother sometimes complained of those he brought home – an abandoned fledgling, the frog he wanted to keep in the bathroom, and most of all the mouse that was making a nest in one of his bedroom drawers. He had wired off a small corner of Juniper's shed and filled it with straw, as a temporary shelter for any hurt thing. The gate between the two fields had long been left open so that both animals could have shelter if they needed it, and they both took an interest in the things they found there, such as the dazed hedgehog that Colin had found by the roadside, and later an exhausted carrier pigeon. Once there had been a starling with an injured leg that he'd managed to splint with a matchstick.

One afternoon Colin was exploring the bank of a lane for the tracks of small animals. Juniper, left to herself, was contentedly snatching a few mouthfuls from the hedge.

Unexpectedly, from beyond the next bend of the lane, ugly sounds broke out. A gate creaked open, boots scraped on the stony path. The growl of voices changed to jeers and laughter, and across them came a shrill whine that ended in a series of piercing yelps. The pain or terror in them cut like a knife-blade across the quiet sunny afternoon.

Colin leaped down from the bank and caught at Juniper's bridle. She could feel his hand trembling slightly as it touched her neck and she sensed his nervousness. The voices were those of boys much older than himself. But he knew an animal needed him. So, leading Juniper, he hurried ahead.

Standing in a gateway were two big boys. Just as he reached them, one of them hurled a stone at a small white object a few yards away in the field. The thing ran a little distance, whimpering, then tried to turn back. The other boy raised his arm too, then stared down in astonishment as two hands grabbed and shook it.

'Stop it! Stop it!' shouted Colin. His face was white and set with rage. 'What d'you think you're doing? Stop it!'

The boy shook him off roughly.

'None of your business, is it? Get out of the way, kid.'

'It's cruel,' gasped Colin. 'You'll kill it. I won't let you.'

'Oh yeah. And how can you stop us?' growled the boy. 'It's our own pup, isn't it? Our Dad don't want it but it keeps coming back.'

'Get rid of it, he says, and we're doing it, see,' said the other. 'So you just clear out and mind your own business.'

He stooped for another stone. Fury left Colin no time to be frightened. He hurled himself at the bully and sent him sprawling by his unexpected attack. But the other grabbed him, swung him round, and hit him so hard in the face that he staggered back into the ditch.

Juniper had watched, afraid of the loud angry voices like those she first remembered, and almost ready to bolt. But something very odd happened to her when she saw Colin fall. For the first time in her life she was seized with anger, a rebellious rage that drove out every other feeling. With a hideous bray she lunged forward, huge mouth yawning, lips drawn back over strong yellow teeth. Her jaws closed on the shoulder of Colin's attacker while she bucked and lashed out with her hind legs at the other as he scrambled up. Colin was struggling from the

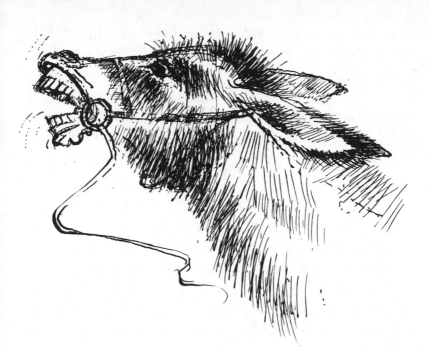

ditch, fiercely wielding a broken branch he had
found there.

It was too much for the enemy. Wrenching
free, they leaped the stile into the opposite field
and set off at a run, shouting threats and insults
over their shoulders. Colin watched them go,
feeling a glow of triumph, then suddenly clung
to Juniper's neck for support. Now that the
battle was over he was trembling. A bruise was
already swelling on his cheek and forehead, and
blood ran from his lip.

'Thanks, oh thanks, chum!' he said with
rather a shaky laugh. 'You showed them, didn't

you. I never thought *you* could show temper! Oh good girl, Juniper. Come on, let's have a look at that pup.'

The puppy wasn't easy to catch. It was limping badly but scurried out of reach whenever he got near it. But slowly it responded to the coaxing voice, sniffed at Colin's fingers and at last allowed itself to be picked up. As his hands closed round it, it yelped and struggled. One leg was obviously hurt. Juniper put her velvet nose gently against the shivering little body. She knew what it was to be scared and in pain.

'It's a little Jack Russell,' said Colin. 'Thank goodness we were there just then. I don't know how badly he's hurt. We'd better get him straight to the vet.'

He thought for a minute, wondering how to hold the puppy comfortably while he mounted. He knew it ought to be moved as little as possible. Then he pulled off his jersey, pushed two strong straight bits of wood inside it along each seam, and tied the arms so that they made a sort of looped handle. He couldn't help wondering what his mother would say. But now he had a sort of very small stretcher that would hang round his neck, and he laid the puppy very carefully inside it. It protected it from too much jolting as Juniper trotted back to the town.

They went straight to the vet's and were in

luck. Miss Thorne was setting out on her afternoon visits, but had only just left the house. She took one look at Colin's face and turned back.

'Come in,' she said. 'I don't know what you've got for me there this time, Colin, but you need a bit of first aid yourself.'

Juniper waited patiently outside, untethered. As long as Colin was near it would never occur to her to stray. In a little while her friends came out again. The blood and dirt had been cleaned from Colin's face and he looked reasonably tidy.

'I'll keep the puppy tonight,' said Miss Thorne, 'and bring him over in the morning. That will give you time to talk to your mother. If she can't take him, we'll find another home for him, don't worry.'

'Are you sure he's all right?' asked Colin.

'Yes. As I told you, there's no fracture, only bad bruising. He'll be fine in a few days.'

Colin sighed with relief as he remounted Juniper.

'Thanks awfully, Miss Thorne.'

They had gone a few paces down the road when the vet called after them.

'Colin. Do you still want to be a vet one day?'

He turned to look back.

'More than anything.'

'Come and see me as soon as the holiday starts. I'll have some jobs for you.'

Colin went red to the ears with excitement.

'Oh, *thanks!*' he shouted. And kicked Juniper so joyfully that she broke into a trot.

CHAPTER SEVEN

Kidnapped

Colin's mother exclaimed over his bruised face, over the state of his jersey, and over the idea of a new puppy to train. But she couldn't resist the wriggling little object that Miss Thorne brought over next day. In no time at all Little Joe was a member of the household and a frequent visitor to the field. Juniper and Hector liked him. When he yapped at their heels they knew it was only infant excitement, and weren't worried.

Hector was very careful not to step on him with his huge feet. People would often stop by the roadside to smile at the oddly assorted trio and the animals grew used to the interest of strangers.

Quite late one spring evening a car drove past and then stopped. Two men got out and came to the gate. They stroked Juniper's nose and patted her neck and said friendly words. But somehow the voices didn't sound as nice as the words. Juniper felt uneasy. She swung her head away so that they couldn't reach over the gate to touch her.

'What do you think?' said one of the men.

'Good bone. Young. Seems quiet. Just what we want, I guess,' said the other.

They went back to their car and drove away. Juniper was glad that they had gone.

A day or two later she was asleep in her favourite corner near the gate when unexpected sounds woke her. She lifted her head, ears pricked.

A van was drawing up close by, though she could see no lights. The night was very dark and she knew it was late. A van door opened and closed very quietly. A man's voice spoke in a whisper, and the gate creaked under someone's weight.

Suddenly nervous, Juniper scrambled to her

feet. Two men were in the field, quite close to her. A beam of torchlight swept to and fro across the grass. The little donkey shifted her weight, ready to bolt, and mud squelched under her feet.

Instantly the torch swung round.

'There she is,' said one of the men softly.

The bright light shone straight into her eyes so that for a moment she was totally blinded. And the moment was too long. A powerful arm gripped her round the neck and a looped rope slid over her head. She opened her mouth to bray out her fear and anger, but hands closed savagely over her muzzle. There was a sharp stabbing pain in her neck. Her head began to swim, her knees buckled, and she felt herself falling into a darkness darker than the night itself.

She woke a long time later, but still in darkness. There was no grass beneath her, only something as hard as the road. But it couldn't be a road because it kept swaying and jolting. She felt sick and very thirsty. There was unfamiliar noise all round her. Feeling scared and ill she tried to get to her feet.

At first her legs folded beneath her again. But at the fifth attempt she got up shakily, only to be thrown sideways. She struck her side painfully against something like a hard wall. Terrified now, she began to kick and plunge, only to bruise herself again and again on the walls of her prison. Once she caught her foot in the rope and fell. She brayed at the top of her voice, but it seemed there was no one to hear. The noise and the swaying and the jolting still went on. At last she collapsed from sheer exhaustion and lay on her side with heaving flanks.

Then quite suddenly it was all over. The floor ceased to move beneath her, the noise stopped. In the unexpected silence she heard footsteps outside her prison, the rattle of bolts, and the darkness gave way abruptly to the level sunshine of early morning.

Someone was standing beside her and a tug of the rope brought her to her feet.

'All over. Come on, now.'

The voice wasn't unkind. But her hooves struck wood that was sloping and hollow. She braced herself rigidly, terrified to set foot on it. The man pulled hard on the rope and his companion climbed up and pushed her from behind. Too tired to resist any more, she slipped and slithered downwards and found herself at last on firm ground. One of her captors brought her a bucket of water and she drank long and thirstily. Then he led her a few yards down a sandy lane, opened a field gate, drove her in, and left her.

It seemed a quiet place. In time she felt

stronger and less afraid. She even felt hungry and began to graze.

Somewhere not far away was an unfamiliar noise – a continuous murmur and a repeated shushing scraping sound that came and went. The air smelled strange too, with a sharp salty tang in it. She looked towards it across the rough tussocky field.

Her heart missed a beat.

There were three other animals on the far side of the field. Donkeys! Except her mother, Juniper had never before seen one of her own kind. She shivered with excitement. They hadn't seen her. Hesitantly she trotted forward, then stopped a few yards away.

A big brown fellow lifted his head and stared at her. Juniper shifted her feet nervously. All three moved towards her, suspicious and inquisitive.

'What's *she* doing here?' demanded the dark grey one.

'Stranger!' snapped the brown donkey.

He came close, then suddenly nipped her flank.

Startled, Juniper broke away and galloped off round the field, chased by the two male donkeys. After a breathless race, the third donkey checked her. She was older than the others, and her sad eyes reminded Juniper of her mother.

'Don't let them bother you,' she said placidly. 'Woody's just a silly show-off and Jacko copies him. They don't mean any harm. They'll soon be used to you.'

The other donkeys joined them peacefully enough, having run off their first aggression. They were both breathing rather hard, their coats were neglected and their sides rather too thin. They weren't in good shape for much galloping.

'Stupids!' said their friend, without temper. 'You'll have quite enough work today. Why don't you rest while you can instead of being so rude?'

'She's a stranger,' grumbled the brown donkey, still suspiciously.

He still looked ready to kick and Juniper backed hurriedly.

'She can't help that, I suppose. We were strangers ourselves once.' The grey donkey's tone was a bit more friendly. 'I'm Jacko. Who are you?'

Juniper felt encouraged. 'I'm Juniper.'

'And I'm Meg,' said the she-donkey. 'And that's Woody. Now we all know each other.'

Woody snorted. 'Where do you come from?' he demanded.

Juniper thought of her own field at home. She was scared and tired and hungry. At home there would have been hay or even bran mash when she needed comfort, loving hands and voices, and big friendly Hector and Little Joe for company. A great desolation overwhelmed her.

'I don't know,' she said sadly. 'It was a lovely place. But those men came. And then I was in a big dark box that moved horribly and made a noise. I don't know where I am. And I want to go home.'

'Bad luck! Nasty!' said Woody, suddenly friendly. 'I was in one of those once. It was awful.'

'Don't take on so,' Meg told her kindly. 'It's not really so bad here. Or not often. I've known worse. You'll get used to it.'

'But where is it?' begged Juniper. 'What do I have to get used to? And what's that queer noise I can hear all the time?'

'Bless you, it's only the sea,' said Jacko. 'Haven't you ever heard it before? We're beach donkeys.'

CHAPTER EIGHT

Beach Donkey

Juniper was puzzled. But she found out only too soon what a beach donkey is.

The sun was high, cheering her a little with its warmth, when the two men came back to the field.

'Best put the new one with Jacko, Harry,' said the tall one. 'He won't fuss too much.'

'All right. I'll lead the others in front in case she plays up. The old saddle in the shed ought to do for her, Dave.'

'Don't try to fuss,' Jacko warned Juniper quietly. 'They'll win anyway. The less you fight them the less trouble you'll get.'

So Juniper stood still while Dave held her headstall with one hand and Jacko's with the other, and they followed him quietly enough. They stopped at a shed a little way down the sandy lane. Juniper pricked her ears hopefully. Perhaps there was hay inside. But Dave led her into a bare empty space with a hard dirt floor. Neglected-looking tack hung on the walls and a worn saddle lay in one corner. He took it up, dropped it over her back, and fastened the girths. Juniper shifted uneasily. The saddle didn't fit very well, and there was a bare patch in the lining that rubbed uncomfortably.

'Stand still, won't you?' snapped Dave impatiently.

He took down a bridle and finished his job with quick rough movements. In a few minutes he had saddled Jacko as well and was leading them out along the lane. The strange shushing sound grew near and louder, the sand became thicker and softer under their feet. The hedges on either side ended at the top of a steep slope where her feet sank and slipped, and the view in front of her suddenly appeared.

There was sand – an enormous stretch of sand ahead and on either side. And beyond the sand was an even more enormous stretch of water that seemed never still. It heaved and glittered as far as she could see until it met the sky, and at the nearer edge it made sudden noisy rushes towards them. Dave was actually leading them down to meet it!

Juniper panicked. She stood still, braced her forelegs against the slope, and tried to back. Dave whacked her hard on the rump, and she opened her mouth wide to bray a protest. Dave hit her again, and she swerved and cannoned sideways into Jacko. He gave her a sharp nip.

'For goodness sake, it's only sea,' he snapped irritably. 'Don't make such a fuss.'

Bewildered and still weak from the terrors of her journey, she was forced down the slope and on to firmer sand. Almost at once children gathered round them.

'Look, there's a new one!'

'Isn't it pretty?'

'What's she called?'

'Bags the first ride.'

'No, me. I saw her first.'

'Now then, no need to fight about it,' said Dave. 'You'll all have a turn in good time. She's called Molly.'

I'm not, I'm not, thought Juniper unhappily. She was worried by so many people round her, all staring and pushing, and so many hands all trying to pat her at the same time. If only one of them was Colin! If only he'd come to take her home!

But there was no Colin. Only, now, a small plump girl who straddled her, kicking impatient heels into her sides.

'Go on, Molly! Go on!'

Dave tugged at the lead rein and she had to follow. The little girl squealed and slipped about. She grabbed painfully at her mount's short tufted mane, but still kicked her to go faster until she broke into a trot. Further along the beach they passed Meg and Woody, also surrounded by children. Meg brayed encouragement and Juniper felt better for it.

It was a morning she would never forget. She grew gradually less afraid of the rushing water, learning slowly that it kept at a distance. At first it seemed to come nearer and then to go further away, but she was never taken very close to it. Again and again she trotted forward and back along the same stretch of beach, until she turned at the right spot without being told. At each return one child scrambled down and another scrambled or was lifted up. Some stroked her and talked to her and sat quietly when they were mounted. They made her almost more homesick for Colin. Others shouted and kicked and pulled painfully at the bit.

Jacko worked nearly as hard as she did. But many of the children wanted 'the new donkey', so that sometimes he was able to stand and rest for a few minutes. Juniper knew that Dave was getting tired, too. Sometimes he let the older riders go on their own while he sat and waited for them.

The sun grew hotter and the morning seemed endless. But at last people began to leave the

beach, while others called their children to eat a picnic. Harry and Dave led their donkeys up the lane again (Juniper was less nervous now of the shifting sand), and turned them loose in the field. Never had grass tasted so good or felt so cool and welcome to the feet!

The respite was all too short. In a couple of hours they were down on the beach again. This time Harry and Dave, themselves needing a rest, took it in turns to lead the smaller children, so that the donkeys too had an occasional break.

Juniper felt, by evening, that she had never been so weary – not even when she drew the vegetable cart. But there was still the next day to face and the next.

She got used to it in time, as Meg had told

her, though like the others she was always tired. The men were not deliberately cruel to them. But they saw them only as a means of earning money. They never noticed how the donkeys' hooves grew and spread through working on soft sand instead of a hard surface. They were themselves too tired to groom the dusty coats, or to notice or do anything about the sore place that the saddle was making on Juniper's back.

Slowly each long day toiled by until all she could think of were the longed-for evenings in the field, or the occasional blessed times when it was too wet for holiday-makers to come down to the beach. Bit by bit she forgot her old home and Mr Jenkins and Hector and Little Joe. At last she often forgot to think of Colin. They all remained only as a vague ache in some deep part of her mind. But always she remembered dimly that once there had been something else. On the least bad days she told herself that one day she would find it again.

CHAPTER NINE

Donkey Derby

By September many of the summer visitors had gone. The donkeys were glad of it as now they sometimes had a rest between rides. But their owners were anxious. They trudged home at the end of each day almost as depressed and tired as the donkeys themselves.

'The season's closing too early,' grumbled Dave. 'We'll have to think of something to get more business.'

'What about a Donkey Derby?' suggested Harry. 'We did quite well on that last year.'

'We ought to have thought of that on Bank Holiday. But maybe there are still enough people about. I suppose we could try it.'

Juniper felt Jacko shiver beside her, and Meg's head drooped even lower than usual. But she put off asking any questions until they were alone in the field.

They had been moved into this field recently

when there was almost no grazing left in the other. There was more grass here, but Juniper was less happy. It was almost at the edge of the beach, with a wire fence instead of a hedge. When the wind set in from the sea it chilled to the bone.

'What's a Donkey Derby?' asked Juniper at last.

'Horrible,' said Woody. 'They make us race each other.'

'And some of those kids have heels as hard and sharp as stirrup irons,' added Jacko.

'It makes my sides ache to remember the last one,' said Meg gloomily.

It didn't seem a cheerful prospect.

Next day there were posters at the top of the beach to advertise 'Harry and Dave's Famous Donkey Derby' to begin at two o'clock on Monday afternoon. For once the donkeys were left to themselves on Monday morning while Dave and Harry put up poles and hung a line of bunting between them. They made a finishing line in the same way at the other end of the beach. The bunting was worn and a bit dirty, but it looked quite gay from a distance. Then they fixed a big rosette, each in a different colour – blue, green, red, white – to the headband of each donkey before leading them down to the beach. There was already a small crowd waiting for them.

The first two races weren't so bad. They were for children small enough to need a grown-up running beside them. Juniper was younger than the other donkeys and, unlike them, had been in good condition at the beginning of the season. She easily won both races.

The next race was for mothers only. There was a lot of laughter among the visitors while four riders were helped to mount. Juniper's was the biggest of all, a fat cheerful woman whose feet almost touched the ground. Juniper felt as if her back would break under the weight and at first couldn't move at all.

There were shouts of 'Gee-up' all round her. Dave whacked her hard on the rump, men and boys pushed her from behind, and the woman laughed and laughed. At last, pulled from one end and pushed from the other, Juniper managed a few staggering steps, got her balance, and began to walk. Worried and confused as she was by all the noise and people round her, she still tried heroically to go faster. But her burden was too heavy. She finished far behind the others, trembling and sweating with exhaustion.

With each race the finishing line seemed further and further away, and all four donkeys found it increasingly hard to trot over the churned-up sand.

The last race was for children over ten years.

Juniper felt anxious the moment she saw her rider. He was a thin, long-legged boy of about thirteen. He was carrying a heavy lump of seaweed in one hand, the kind like a short thick rope with a cluster of brown streamers at the end. He mounted carelessly, jerking painfully at the bit, and yelled and kicked her hard as they started.

Still doggedly doing her best, Juniper forced herself into a trot. But it wasn't fast enough for her rider. He went on kicking viciously, and now he began to thrash her with the seaweed. The stem of it was hard enough to hurt like a stick. The sore place under her saddle was becoming unbearable as he bounced on it. He struck her on the neck and suddenly the wet streamers lashed blindingly across her eyes. Bewildered and in pain, Juniper whirled sharply aside, plunging and kicking to free herself from this unknown terror. The boy lost his balance, slithered, and then shot off over her head. She broke into a desperate gallop until someone ran out in front of her and caught her bridle. The boy scrambled up and joined them, giving her a savage punch. There was a bruise on his face where he had hit it against a stone.

'You vicious little brute! I'll teach you to do that again!'

He raised his arm threateningly. But the man

who had caught Juniper grabbed it and pulled him back.

'No, you don't. It was your fault. I saw what you were doing. Oafs like you aren't fit to be near an animal.' He turned to Dave who had just joined them. 'Don't blame the donkey. This lad got what he well deserved. And it's time this poor creature had a rest.'

'She's well enough,' said Dave defensively. 'It was the last race anyway.'

'She hurt me,' complained the boy, touching his bruised cheek cautiously. 'I hit my shoulder as well. Perhaps I've broken something.'

'You'll have worse than that if you beat one of my donkeys again,' growled Dave. 'Be off with you.'

The boy said something rude under his breath, but walked sullenly away. Dave thanked the man for his help and led Juniper back to the starting place. It had indeed been the last race. Harry had already put away the day's takings and was folding up the bunting, and soon they were all plodding up from the beach.

As the evening grew darker, Meg, Jacko and Woody lay down one by one and settled thankfully to sleep. But Juniper was still restless. She ached all over and the sore place on her back worried her badly. She wandered to the far side of the field and stood fidgeting by the wire fence. The wind had changed with the coming of night. It blew from inland, bringing soft sweet smells that Juniper had almost forgotten – not the salt bitter smell of the sea, but scents of trees and rich pasture, of ripening fruit and woodsmoke. Comfortable country smells.

Juniper lifted her tired head to sniff the air. It reminded her of things almost forgotten, things that stirred deep in her mind, dim memories of peaceful pasture, of good hay, of loving hands and kind voices.

She moved closer to the fence, pressing against it in her eagerness to catch those alluring smells. The wire moved under the weight of her body. And the movement brought another memory. She scraped a restless foot in the sandy soil. The earth fell away until soon there was a deeper space below the bottom strand of wire. Juniper lay down and rolled. The wire bent upwards above her. One of the posts dragged sideways, making it still slacker.

Juniper gave a final kick and roll. Next minute she had scrambled to her feet, stood a moment to catch the scent of the wind again, and then trotted off into the dark. She was out on the open common, heading for the nearly remembered something else.

CHAPTER TEN

Runaway

By next day Juniper was already quite a long way from the coast. Sometimes she stopped to eat or rest, but always wandered northwards. The common on to which she had escaped stretched on and became part of the rising moorland behind it. There were patches of bright green grass between rough gorse and heather. They looked inviting, but Juniper quickly learned that the ground in such places was often boggy and dangerous. She was uneasy in such unfamiliar country. But she was glad to find no roads, only a few tracks across the moor. There were no cars and no people, so she felt she might be safe here from Dave and Harry and their van. She didn't know, of course, that they daren't make too many inquiries about a donkey that they themselves had stolen.

The moorland seemed to go on for ever. She longed for familiar fields and hills. Pictures of

Colin grew clearer in her mind as she began to remember his smell and touch and voice. But for a few days she was happy just to be free, to have no burdens to carry, no sticks to fear. Her body ached less. The sore rubbed patch began to heal. Once she came upon a farmhouse, near enough to hear the barking of dogs. But she turned away at once, heading for higher and more desolate ground. She thought of her mother's words – 'Never expect anything from people, then you won't be disappointed'. But she knew she'd been luckier than her mother. Colin and his father had been kind, but she also knew now that the warning had been wise. She would never again trust strangers.

In October came days of heavy rain and violent wind. There was little shelter in all that desolation. Juniper was lonely with only clouds and birds and rabbits for company. Then one day she caught a fresh smell, but one that she remembered. She stood quite still, sniffing the air. Dim pictures stirred in her mind of stolid cheerful little Tinker and big friendly Hector. She trotted hopefully forward, peering through the mist and driving rain.

There they were. Ponies! Several mares and yearlings and a sturdy brown stallion. Driven by loneliness, and hopeful by nature, Juniper stepped delicately towards them.

At once the whole herd stopped feeding. They raised their heads and moved closer together. The mares might have let her get near. But the stallion neighed a warning on a high angry note. Juniper stood still.

'Please,' she said anxiously. 'I don't want to disturb you. But I'm all on my own. And I haven't seen anyone to talk to for days and days. And – and – if you'd just let me . . .'

She got no further. The stallion stamped his front feet, screamed, and charged.

Juniper turned and fled, but he was already on her. His teeth closed on her neck and she felt a vicious kick on her foreleg as she struggled to break away. In a minute she was free, galloping as fast as her small slim legs would stretch. The stallion chased her for a short distance, then lost interest and went back to his mares. But Juniper galloped almost to exhaustion before she dared to stop.

The ponies were long out of sight. She was alone again among the gorse and heather, trembling and sweating with effort. Her bruised foreleg, already swelling, hurt her when she moved. Flies, attracted by the oozing blood, tormented her, settling in buzzing clouds on the bite mark on her neck. There was no way she could reach them, no tree against which she could rub them off.

Each day now her loneliness increased. Once or twice she saw other groups of ponies, but she took care to keep her distance from them. She came across a few sheep here and there, but they ignored her as if she weren't there at all. Her injured leg had stiffened so much that walking was difficult, but still she kept moving northwards. The grazing was poor, but in any case she had no wish to eat much. The bite on her neck burned and throbbed but her body felt cold, and sometimes there seemed to be a fire inside her head. There was something wrong with her sight too. Objects came and went before her eyes, sometimes too close and sometimes too small and far away. Above all she was troubled by thirst.

Some miles back there had been a small clear stream of water. She remembered it longingly, but it was too far to go back to look for it. She had no strength left.

Late in the afternoon she reached the edge of the moor and staggered feebly down the last grassy slope in which it ended. She reached a lane, a group of farm buildings. She was too ill now to care where she was or to remember her fear of people. She was aware of nothing but pain and thirst.

On the far side of the lane were iron railings and a gate. And beyond the gate was a big tank

into which a tap was gently dripping. With one last effort she reached the gate and fell.

After that everything seemed a jumble between snatches of darkness and dream. People came and went near her. There were hands that felt her, gently exploring her injuries. Voices spoke above her, but she was too tired to try to understand. She knew dimly that she was lifted on to something, taken up and carried. Water. Darkness again. Fresh clean straw. Voices now that soothed, hands that gentled, something that eased the burning pain in her neck. A long strange confusion in which only two things mattered – she was no longer alone and no longer afraid.

CHAPTER ELEVEN

Alice

Many days later Juniper stood at the door of her loose box, gazing out across the farmyard. She was filled with deep content. She had a loose box all to herself, with fresh straw to lie on, good hay to eat, and sometimes still a warm bran mash like those that had coaxed her to eat again after her illness. She had learned to trust Mr Allen, who owned the farm. He was always gentle with her, and so was Robert the cowman who often looked after her.

It was a warm still day of late autumn. Juniper heard Mr Allen's voice and then a child's voice in answer. The farmer appeared round the corner of the barn, carrying a little girl in his arms. He brought her over to the donkey's stall.

'There she is, Alice,' he said. With his free hand he gave a friendly rub to Juniper's ears. 'See how quiet and gentle she is. She's going to be your special friend. Give her a pat.'

But the little girl leaned back, clinging to him. She was about the same age as Colin, but fair and pale. Her thin small body looked fragile, and Juniper sensed fear in her. From a grown-up she would have caught the same fear and been restless. But the child was so slight and frail that the little donkey felt only sympathy. Stretching her head over the half door, she pushed her nose gently against the small feeble hand.

'There!' said her father. 'She wants to be friends with you. Don't be nervous, Alice. She won't hurt you.'

The child's face lit with a sudden smile that transformed it. She leaned from her father's arms and, still a bit nervously, patted Juniper's silver nose. The donkey's ears twitched forward in response.

'She likes me,' said Alice happily.

That was the first of many visits. Alice came each day, often bringing tit-bits which she offered with increasing confidence. Soon her father brought her into the loose box and set her down on a clean pile of straw. Juniper was at first puzzled that she sat there so quietly. The children she had met would all want to be busy and active, dashing from one thing to another. But at last she realised that Alice was unable to walk alone. She could stagger a few steps if her father held both her hands, but even that made

her tired. Juniper felt very protective towards her.

She still remembered that her real name was Juniper, but Alice called her Silver.

Between these visits she was often let out into a paddock near the house. It was a joy to gallop freely again. Her sores and bruises were completely healed, and hair began to cover the scar on her neck. Her hooves had been trimmed, and she would often race round the paddock out of a sheer sense of well-being. Every day she looked forward to her meetings with Alice.

One morning Mr Allen came into her box with a small saddle and bridle. Juniper watched him anxiously, but he spoke and moved so quietly that she felt reassured. The saddle was light and had a raised support for the rider's back. Mr Allen fitted it carefully before leading her out into the paddock. Alice was already there, this time in her mother's arms. Juniper had seen Mrs Allen only rarely, but was happy with her. She was a brisk, busy person, with little time left for the stables, but she was always kind.

The farmer kept one hand on the little donkey's bridle. With the other he steadied Alice as her mother lifted her to the saddle and fastened a small strap to support her against its high back.

'It's all right, darling. I'm holding you too. You can't possibly fall off.'

A memory stirred in Juniper of the joyful rides she had once shared with Colin. Alice was much lighter. She sat in a little heap instead of upright, and Juniper could feel that she was trembling.

Mr Allen pulled gently at the bridle.

'Move on, Silver.'

Juniper moved forward slowly and carefully, trying to take special care of her little rider.

'Good girl!' said Mr Allen.

Juniper didn't know if he spoke to her or Alice. But in a minute or two she felt the child relax and sit more firmly. In response she walked a little more quickly.

'Daddy, look!'

Alice was upright. Juniper felt the difference and sensed the sudden confidence in the hands that lay on her neck. Happiness flowed warmly between her and her rider.

They walked all round the paddock. Then Mrs Allen unfastened the belt and lifted her daughter down. Alice's eyes were shining with excitement, and there was actually a touch of colour in her pale cheeks. She leaned forward from her mother's arms to clasp Juniper's neck and rub her face against it.

'Thank you, Silver. Oh, I do love you!' Then

her face suddenly clouded. 'Daddy, you only *found* Silver, didn't you? Suppose she belongs to someone? Suppose they want her back?'

'Don't worry, love. We advertised her in the papers, and I told all the local vets. No one's come forward to claim her in all these weeks. She's safely yours now.'

Alice gave a sigh of relief.

'I won't let her go,' she said. 'Not ever, ever.'

Every fine day after that she came out to ride. Each time she sat more firmly and was soon brave enough for a gentle trot. She was certainly growing stronger. Juniper came to love her and looked forward to their times together. Now that she herself was well fed and cared for she was often frisky and sometimes naughty. But with Alice she was always careful and quiet, endlessly patient.

For a long happy year their friendship grew. Juniper was proud to be trusted and to be able to help. So she was very surprised when, one day, Alice didn't want to ride.

'But why not, darling?' asked her mother. 'You know you always love it.'

'I'm tired,' complained Alice. 'My head aches.'

'But riding does you so much good. Go just a little way,' coaxed Mrs Allen. 'Then you can take a rest.'

Her father lifted her to the saddle. But Juniper knew at once that there was something wrong. Alice sat limply, just as she had on that first ride. She clung to the donkey's neck with small hot hands, and Juniper felt her distress. She walked on with more than usual care, trying to help her rider's balance.

'It's almost as if Silver knows, isn't it?' said Mr Allen, patting her gratefully.

But Alice wanted almost at once to get down. She stroked her friend as usual but seemed quite glad to leave her and go indoors. Juniper watched sadly as she was carried back to the house.

Next day the child seemed better. But the day after that she was tired and listless again, and complained that her head hurt. Juniper waited for her hopefully all the next morning, but she never came.

All that week Juniper stayed alone in her loose box. Once or twice she saw Mr Allen, but he looked worried and preoccupied and didn't come near her. Robert the cowman looked after her, but he seemed unhappy. He fed and watered her, but it seemed that no one had time any more to talk to her. Day after day she waited, staring out of her loose box, feeling sad and neglected. But Alice never came.

CHAPTER TWELVE

Lydd Fair

Two weeks passed, then Juniper was turned out into the paddock again. Her spirits rose and she raced round it at full gallop. Alice must be better. She would surely come this morning and everything would be all right again. But the hours went by and still brought no small friend to see her. Juniper brayed loudly, trotting to the end of the paddock nearest the house. No one took any notice. The windows of the house stared emptily as if there was no one there.

At last she gave up hope. The sun shone and the spring grass was beginning to grow. She began to nibble but had no real heart for it. All day she moped unhappily, sometimes braying her loneliness to the empty field.

It was early spring but the nights were still sharp and frosty. In the evening Robert took her back to her loose box and she was glad to go in. There was sweet hay in the rack and she pulled at it, but without any real interest. Robert looked worried and stayed longer than usual to make a fuss of her. Juniper pushed her grey nose into his shirt for comfort. But when he had gone she lay down without eating.

Another month went by. Juniper no longer hoped to see Alice, but she still thought of her. The paddock felt very empty.

Early one morning as she waited to be let out she heard Mr Allen's footstep in the yard as well as Robert's. They came over and looked at her together. She rarely saw Mr Allen now. He was quieter than he used to be and laughed less easily. But now he stroked her ears and talked to her as kindly as ever. But still she sensed that there was something wrong.

'She's out of condition,' said Mr Allen at last.

'Ah,' agreed Robert. 'I reckon she's been pining. There's nothing else wrong with her.'

Mr Allen nodded. 'She and Alice were such friends. She was bound to miss her. She's idle and lonely and bored, and I've no real job for her.' His hand tightened on the donkey's neck. 'And to tell you the truth, Robert, she reminds me too much of the past. She'll have to go.'

'I'll be sorry for it,' said Robert. 'She's a good little beast.'

'I know. That's why she deserves a better deal. Heaven knows, I'm grateful for what she did for my girl. But she'd be happier in work than moping here on her own. You'd better take her to Lydd Fair on Friday.'

Friday came, and Robert gave Juniper bran mash for breakfast as a special treat. Afterwards he brushed her till her silver coat shone in the sunshine, and led her out into the yard. The farm car was there with the small covered trailer behind it. Mr Allen was there, too, and made a great fuss of her. His sadness made her feel sad herself. The ramp of the trailer was down and Robert coaxed her up it.

Juniper was suddenly afraid. The wood trembled as she stepped on to it and her hooves made a hollow sound. There was a dark closed space ahead of her that made her remember another horrible journey. She brayed in terror and tried to fight her way back. But she was only a little donkey and the two men were too strong for her.

But this journey was not as dreadful as the last. A short tether kept her from plunging, and straw bales on each side of the trailer protected her from hurt. After a while she realised that the noise and movement were harmless and her fear slowly subsided. All the same she was thankful when at last they stopped, and Robert opened the doors and coaxed her out into the open air again.

At first Juniper was wholly bewildered. She found herself in a great open space crowded with animals and people. There were rows of horses tethered in lines and, here and there, a donkey like herself. Men were everywhere, looking at the horses, feeling their legs, looking at their mouths, talking or arguing with each other, calling to their dogs. It was all noise and bustle. Many people crowded round a roped-off space in the middle, where someone was leading a horse round and round.

Robert led Juniper to a place where two or three donkeys were already tethered, and brought her some water. He stayed with her for a while, watching what went on, then walked off to the ring where another horse was now being shown.

Juniper looked at her companions. They took no notice of her. They stood as if bored or tired. But the one next to her looked not too unfriendly. She spoke to him timidly.

'Where are we? What are all those people doing?'

The other donkey snorted with surprise.

'It's Lydd Fair, of course. Haven't you ever been here before?'

'No,' said Juniper unhappily. 'I don't like it. I don't understand it.'

'My goodness!' said her companion. 'You *are*

ignorant, aren't you? We're here for someone to buy us, of course. Cheer up, you may be lucky. I had a nice place last time.'

But poor Juniper found it difficult to cheer up. She wanted only the place she had just left. She was worried by all the noise and movement, and by the strangers who sometimes stopped to stare at her or handle her. Some petted her and spoke kindly, but went on. Others treated her as if she was an object, not a living creature with feelings of her own. But all of them were unknown and made her feel nervous.

Some time later Robert came back to her. He was talking with a short dark man, one of those who had looked at her earlier.

'It's a good choice if you have her,' said Robert. 'As nice a little donkey as you'd find anywhere. Strong and good-tempered. Just what you're after. Used to children too. She's been a family pet. The boss wants a good home for her.'

'She'll get that if I have her,' said the man.

He patted Juniper and smiled. But Juniper sensed no caring in his hands as he felt her legs and back and shoulders. They gripped hard when he pulled her jaws open to look at her teeth. His mouth was still smiling, but she could see no smile in his eyes. Robert led her to and fro, first at a walk, then at a trot, while the man stared at her.

'Hm,' he said at last. 'Well, she might do.'

'You'll not find a better,' said Robert. They walked away a few paces, arguing.

'They always do that,' said Juniper's donkey friend. 'I don't know why. It doesn't mean anything. He'll take you in the end.'

Juniper felt gloomier than ever. Whatever the man said to Robert, she knew there was little

kindness in him. She didn't want to follow when he came back and took her lead rein. Robert gave her a friendly clap on the rump.

'Good luck, Silver. I'll miss you.'

She turned her head round towards him, longing to go home. But her new owner pulled sharply at the rein and she was forced to follow.

They were near the exit when the man

stopped to speak to some friends. Juniper waited, sad and patient. Other people pushed by. A tall dark boy paused close beside her to say goodbye to a companion. He was so near her that she caught the smell of his clothes.

Deep inside Juniper's memory something stirred. She knew that smell. She thrust out her head to get closer to it, nudging the boy's shoulder. He turned to look at her and she saw his face. It was thinner and firmer now than when she had last seen it – a grown boy's face, not a child's. But she knew.

She opened her mouth and brayed with joy. The boy's companion laughed.

'She's talking to you, Colin.'

'Seems like it,' grinned the boy. 'There, there, little 'un.' He fondled her nose and ears with a friendly hand, and was about to move on. Juniper brayed again and tried to follow, tugging desperately at her rope. Her new owner turned.

'Here, stand still, can't you?'

But now the boy had turned round again and was staring at her.

'Is that your donkey?'

'I've just bought her – if it's any of your business.'

'But I think – I think – it *may* be my business. Please, let me look at her. She's just like the donkey I once had myself. Yes, look! The same markings on her face. There can't be two *exactly* like that.' He stepped back, looking at her. 'Juniper! Juniper, is it really you? Juniper?'

Juniper tugged at the rein again, struggling to reach him.

'Well, I never!' said her new owner. 'It looks as if she really does know you.'

'She does, she does!' said the boy joyfully. 'She was stolen from us but I knew she wouldn't forget me. Dad! Dad!' he shouted to someone ahead of him.

A familiar voice answered. 'What is it, son?'

Juniper's skin shivered with delight as she saw the well-remembered figure of her very first friend making its way through the crowd. A little slower and heavier than he used to be, but quite unmistakeably Mr Jenkins. A small white creature dashed suddenly past him, leaped up towards Juniper's nose, then raced in circles round her, barking shrilly.

'Look, Dad, look! It's Juniper! Little Joe knows her too. We've found her!'

'*Found* her? Are you sure?'

'Yes. She's got *exactly* the same markings. She tried to follow me. She knows her name. She knows me, Dad. And look how Little Joe's behaving. It really *is* Juniper.'

Mr Jenkins was beside her now, staring intently. She rubbed her nose against him in an ecstasy of affection.

'Well, I'll be jiggered! I do believe you're right, Colin.'

Juniper's new owner broke in, suspicious and angry.

'Here, what's all this about? What do you mean, she was stolen? I've just bought her, fair and honest.'

'Of course you have,' Mr Jenkins calmed him. 'It's a long time ago that the donkey was stolen. I guess we'll never know what really happened. But it's the same donkey all right. And my son loves her. How much did you pay for her? I'll give you more if you'll let me buy her back.'

The man hesitated and argued. But at last Mr Jenkins got his own way. In a few minutes Juniper was once again inside a van. But this time she was used to it and not afraid. How could she be afraid when Colin and his father were near? And in the straw beside her, all ears to hear her story, and whining with delight, was Little Joe.

When the journey ended she knew exactly where she was. There was the lane, there was her own field, there was the same shed in the corner. And there, best of all, was big Hector and the loving friends that she had known so long.

Juniper had come home.

CHAPTER THIRTEEN

Another Spring

At one end of the field big Hector was cropping the grass, exchanging an occasional word with Little Joe, who was hunting for rabbits in the hedge. Two small figures stood nose to tail under the shadows of the big oak at the other end. Fresh grass rippled under the spring wind.

Juniper turned her head to nuzzle the little grey foal at her side.

'Tell me again,' said the foal.

'I've already told you.'

'But I want to hear it again. All of it.'

So Juniper told it all again, all the story of her life, while the foal listened.

'Will any of those things happen to me?'

'Not the bad ones. I don't think so. We have a safe stable now at night so that no one can steal us. And Colin and his father have said that they'll never, never part with either of us.'

'I'm glad,' said the little foal, pressing close

against her. 'I'd quite like some adventures, but not horrid ones.'

Juniper reached for a nice fat thistle. The sun shone warmly on her back, turning her grey hide to silver. There was a scent of growing things, and a blackbird sang from the hedge. In the distance she could hear Colin's voice and she pricked her ears. She looked at her foal with wise happy eyes.

'I think you will always be happy, my little one. Your home is safe. But if ever any sadness *does* happen, be brave. Remember that beyond all troubles there is always something else. And you will find it.'

Elisabeth Beresford

ARMADA ADVENTURE

An adventure story set against the background of the Spanish Armada, published on its 400th anniversary from top children's author Elisabeth Beresford.

Elisabeth Beresford's exciting adventure story is set in the Channel Islands where several of the ships in the Spanish Armada passed by. It follows the fortunes of Rollon who lives on the small island of Aurney and his long search for his father whom everyone else believes is dead. In a marvellous climax set against the ominous approach of the Spanish galleons, Rollon discovers that his trust has not been misplaced . . .

Elisabeth Beresford

CHARLIE'S ARK

There wasn't a lot Charlie was scared about
except being taken away from life with his
cousins Sula and Nowt and going into care.
To avoid the In Care Man the three of them
decide on a walk – and find themselves in a
part of the city they had never seen before,
where no one else seems to go except for
animals. They also find an old boat. It is the
start of their adventure. An adventure
which even Charlie couldn't have begun to
imagine . . .

Gillian Cross

RESCUING GLORIA

Kevin turned round with his mouth open.
'There's – there's a goat in Rachel's
bathroom.'
But it's just another episode in the chaotic
chain of events which starts when Leo
rescues Gloria from certain death. Where do
you keep a goat when you live in a first-floor
flat – to say nothing of the milking! Rachel
and Harjinder help, but when ducks, hens
and bees land on their doorstep, Leo feels
things are getting a little out of hand . . .

Also by Gillian Cross, winner of the
Whitbread Award, are three entertaining
school stories about Barny, Spag and
Clipper: *Save Our School, The Mintyglo Kid*
and *Swimathon*!

Jamila Gavin

THE HIDEAWAY

The secret cave in the woods is the most important thing in Peter's life. It's his very own kingdom: the one place where he can forget all the troubles at home and at school.

Then he reaches crisis point. He has to get away. And the hideaway is the obvious place to go. So it is that he makes some unexpected and helpful new friends . . .

Alexander McCall Smith

UNCLE GANGSTER

Carlo has always longed to go to faraway and exciting places and is thrilled when he finds that he is on the wrong plane . . . destination New York! He does not expect his adventure to last long so is both surprised and anxious to find that his 'aunt' and 'uncle' are waiting to meet him at the airport.

But when Carlo accidentally finds out about his 'uncle's' strange business activities he longs to go home. But how can he escape? . . .

Derek Sampson

FOLLOW THAT PHAROAH

The twins never did work out exactly how it happened. One moment, the ancient Egyptian had been dead for 3,000 years – and the next he was alive and kicking like a demented doughnut.

Suddenly, Josie and Martin had a pompous, pop-eyed pharaoh on their hands. He bullied their neighbours, played amazing magic tricks and could summon up a plague of frogs without batting an eyelid.

Still, there was nothing else for Josie and Martin to do but grit their teeth, hang on to their socks – and follow that pharaoh!

Richard Severy

ANGEL

Angie and her twin brother, Billy, catch a
steam train to school every day. Their father
is a Signalman on the local railway line. But
things are changing. There are rumours that
the line is going to be closed, and at school
the new headmistress is determined to
believe that Angie is a troublemaker.

Hurt, almost defeated, Angie fights – and
against all the odds she finally triumphs in a
spectacular way.

Ann Turnbull

TROUBLE WITH BATS

'I'm getting old,' Nan said.
'You don't look old,' said Emma.
Nan laughed and said, 'Well, I feel it.
On the outside. Inside I feel just the same as
I did when I was your age – I'm still me, the
same person. The same I was then . . .'

And Emma discovers just what Nan had
been like fifty years ago when Emma's home
had been the farmhouse and the family had
secrets . . .

The special relationship of grandmother and
granddaughter, past and present, is
beautifully brought to life in this new story
from the author of
Summer of the Cats.